Praise For L

"Two delightfully strong female protagonists. One is human; one is AI. The dialogue between them is priceless: sometimes snarky, sometimes comforting, all times entertaining."

Into The Abyss

"Epic SciFi at its best."

Koeur's Book Reviews

"Intelligent science fiction: much, much smarter than your typical run-and-gun sci-fi romp."

High Fever Books

"Thrilling space horror with an unconventional female friendship at the core."

Banshee Irish Horror Blog

"I loved this book. It's fast, scary, dark at times, and features a young woman I grew to admire and root for in her quest."

Brew and Books Review

"A perfect balance of sci-fi and horror. I cannot emphasise how much I loved this book."

Life Of A Nerdish Mum

Afua

Lost Tales Of Solace Book 5

Karl Drinkwater, Christoffer Petersen

Organic Apocalypse

Afua

Cover design by Karl Drinkwater

Published by Organic Apocalypse
ISBN 978-1-911278-46-7 (Ebook)
ISBN 978-1-911278-47-4 (Paperback)

Organic Apocalypse Copyright Manifesto

Organic Apocalypse believes culture should be shared. We support far more reuse than copyright law and licensing organisations currently allow. We respect our buyers, reviewers, libraries and educators.

You can copy or quote up to 50% of our publications, for any non-commercial purpose, as long as the awesome source is acknowledged.

You may sell our print books when you've finished with them. Or pass them on to other people and share the love. You buy a copy, you own it.

We don't add DRM to our e-books. Feel free to convert between formats (including scanning, e-formats, braille, audio) and store a backup for your own use.

Afua

The Ninth Day

The ophanti are my restless ones, and on the ninth day we gather to paint the Dooga.

The day, like most mid-season days, starts with a heavy mist between the trees. The sun turns the mist a cream colour, and the blue spores of pollen that cling to the drops of water are the berries. Berries and cream are the finest way to start any day.

I walk barefoot along the path to the clearing. Barefoot is best, despite what they say in the city. Walking barefoot, I can detect the ripple of ssanju worms in the soil and avoid their spiny tails. I have taught the ophanti this, and since they began leaving their sandals at the forest edge there have been no incidents, no spines to remove. The lighter the foot, the sharper the senses.

"And wings are lightest of all, yes, Akalie?"

I hold up my hand for the fat Dooga and she settles on my palm with a rasping down-draught. Like the ophanti, she belongs to me, but she is not restless. These days, the fatter she grows, the greater her urge to find a broad leaf to curl up inside. She is swollen with baby Dooga – six at last count, when the light caught her belly and I saw the heads through her translucent skin. Dooga, my favourite of all Nuafri fauna, have long abdomens, bobble heads, and right-angle wings. Akalie's legs are hidden in the folds of her belly, but teeth are all the tools she needs to make a nest before pushing her babies out.

Today I will paint her as I have every ninth day for the past season. But she will leave me soon, and my heart grows heavy as she grows fat.

"Will you miss me, I wonder?"

I choose to speak for her, interpreting the flutter of wings as a *yes*, and the dip of her head as *no*. The ripple of her belly in my palm is probably baby gas, but I like to imagine she is laughing.

"Afua! Afua!"

Xanta is the first to spot me, and he has been busy. He holds out his hands to reveal six heavy ovals: litrus nuts, the soft brown fruit, ripe and ready for topping. I check his hands and reward him with a smile.

"Only two blisters this time," I say. "You're improving."

Xanta puts the nuts in the satchel slung across his chest, then mimes the cutting of the litrus nut from the spiny stem on which it grows.

"I curl the leaf around the prickles," he says, demonstrating with an imaginary leaf in his palm. "Two leaves are best, but only when two grow together. Don't cut a leaf to steal a nut."

I still find it strange to hear my words in ophanti mouths. They are shunned by their siblings for selfishness, rejected by schools for their loud behaviour. And yet, here in the woods, they whisper apologies to the roots they crawl over, and take every fourth nut rather than the first they find. All the while they listen for the buzz of the Derago, feel for the wriggle of ssanju worms, and sniff for the Kchak.

"My ophanti," I say, as the rest of the group gather around Xanta.

I count them all; greet them with soft words, the latest – often complex – handshake they invented eight days earlier, and a soft hum as we sing for the Dooga. Akalie flutters her wings, and we search the mist, pointing at the pockets of blue pollen that burst when a Dooga flies through it.

"But where is Tifundu?" I ask, suddenly aware that I have only five ophanti, not six as I expected.

"Sick," Uunta says, giggling as a playful Dooga buzzes her hair.

"Grumpy," says a small boy I think might be Jatta. His twin brother Archa nods in agreement and I see the scar on Archa's chin and can now tell them apart.

"He's not grumpy, and he's not sick."

Trust Eleena to put them all right. We've talked about this, but her manner is softer than it once was, and I have learned to listen to her as she often sees what others don't.

"Tell me," I say, as the twins chase the Dooga over roots and around stumps.

"He went for a long walk yesterday," Eleena says. She is barely nine years old but wears the frown of a village elder. She will make a good one, too, if she is allowed to take the diplomatic training required for Filiates. "I said he shouldn't go alone, but you know what he's like."

Yes, I do. Tifundu is all brawn with just enough brain to get into trouble, but never enough to get out of it again.

"And where did he go?"

Eleena thrusts her arm in front of her body, so fast and straight I think she has been waiting for me to ask, so she can be the one to point the way.

"And for how far?"

"He was gone half the day," she says. "I didn't see him come back again."

"Yesterday?"

"That's right," she says. "The day before today."

I know the path Tifundu took. I often go that way when I want to meditate undisturbed. There are ruins and steep escarpments half a day along the route, and even more wildly rifted earth just beyond. But my thinking never takes me further than the ruins before I must return.

"Afua," Xanta says. He lifts the flap of his satchel, then drops it quickly as a Dooga flies in for a closer look.

"Yes," I reply.

Tifundu will have to wait. It is time to paint the Dooga.

"Fly high, Akalie," I say, lifting my palm and bouncing her into the air.

The ophanti gather around me, and I make fists, shushing the young Nuafri with my eyes. I press my fingers tight, feeling for my pulse, counting ten beats before clapping my hands. It is an old trick, one of the first I learned when I was old enough to receive my subcutaneous palm pads. The pads charge with the beat of my heart and ten beats give enough energy to disperse and disorientate a cloud of Dooga when I clap. Fifteen beats will knock them out, and even kill a Derago, the smaller, deadlier cousin of the Dooga. But I have yet to meet anyone my age who can wait for fifteen steady beats when a Derago settles on their nose.

"Afua!"

I am distracted today. It must be Tifundu and the ruins stealing my thoughts. Xanta jogs me back into the moment with a litrus nut in one hand and a knife in the other, but he won't slice it before I say so.

I nod for him to cut, and then ask, "Who has the spores?"

"Red," says Uunta. She removes a wooden cup from the pocket of her long shirt. The lid slides to one side, revealing a generous collection of crimson pollen.

"I have yellow."

Yellow is my favourite, and Archa knows it. He always collects yellow.

"Green," says Eleena.

"I found kirant," Jatta says.

"Kirant?" I am surprised and step closer to see what Jatta has in his wooden cup. Kirant is the deepest of woodland shades, almost as dark as our skin, but streaked with a brilliant light. "You know what you get if you mix that, Jatta?"

"Mix it with yellow," he says, "and you have to slit your eyes like this."

Eleena laughs, and Jatta chases her until he realises that he is spilling his precious pollen.

Xanta cuts the tops of the litrus nuts. They are fruits, really, and the translucent slick inside mixes into a coloured paste with the spores my ophanti have collected. Of course, the smell is ridiculous, but after many ninth days in a row, we no longer care.

I used to be the one to help them mix the paint, but now it is Xanta. It is quite remarkable how he has changed since we met on the first ninth day. He and Tifundu were the brawniest and dumbest of the group – the most restless. But here he is, sharing out the juice of the litrus nut, pouring a generous glob into each of the ophanti's left hands.

Right hands are for dusting. Eleena starts with green, the colour of the woods, our base colour. Today, everyone is eager for a dusting of Jatta's kirant. We might have experimented with more subtle blends, but the vibrant shock of kirant, when mixed with greens, yellows, and reds, makes fire in our palms.

Mine burn yellow after mixing it with the children's spoils, and I hope Akalie is as excited as I am.

"Remember to cup your palm," I say. "Don't grab when the Dooga lands."

"We know," they say, and they do. They are proficient at this now.

Xanta hurries to mix his paint as the others hold their cupped palms high. The Dooga have recovered from the mild shock of my clap, and they buzz the ophanti, settling on one palm, before taking off to splash onto another.

I remind the ophanti of the chemical tickle the Dooga experience when coating their abdomens with litrus paint. I tell them the old word *nectar*, and explain its many meanings, not least that of ecstasy. Yes, that word is the best way to describe the reactions of the Dooga when they take painted flight.

Akalie is slower to visit my palm, and I wonder if she is thinking of her babies? But then she lands, rolls, and dips her bobble head with its single compound eye.

"Are you going to get fat?" Uunta asks me.

"Oh, yes. I want to be so fat I will have six."

"Six what?" she asks, and the others tilt their heads to listen.

They know the answer already, but I tell them again, because I love the giggles and snickers that erupt when I say, "Six ophanti! Just like you."

"And will you look after them?" Archa asks, as he removes globs of paint from the wings of a greedy Dooga. "Will you be there for them when they need you?"

"No," I say, because it is expected. "Not at all. Only every nine days."

"And what will they do for the other eight?"

Eleena is serious, and I must be careful. Luckily, Akalie is ready to take flight, and I can slip my arm around Eleena's bony shoulders.

"They will run in the woods, chasing Dooga and eating ssanju worms."

"They can't," she says.

"They can. Just like you."

Xanta butts in, excited now, and covered in litrus juice. "Do it," he says. "We are all ready."

I wipe my hands on the front of my patterned tunic, shaking my head at the mess. It is dull as there is no heat. Litrus paint is best warm, better when heated, and when I charge my palm pads – three beats, three claps, recharge and repeat – the Dooga run hot, like tiny torsion drives. Their litrus-painted bodies flash through the haze. It's what we look forward to every ninth day – even me. It never grows old.

But today, with Jatta's kirant spores mixed in our litrus paints, the Dooga streak faster than rockets. We squint at them, pointing and shrieking as the Dooga buzz our hands for more nectar.

Akalie buzzes with them, and I am glad she is not quite ready to leave me. I will miss her, and am determined to enjoy every last moment together.

I only wish Tifundu were here to see it, too.

He is one of my ophanti, and his absence makes me restless.

The Path To The Ruins

Tifundu is from the city. He is as tough as the vine-crossed streets he grew up on, but little more than a blight on the image the Nuafri wish to portray.

"I am Nuafri."

I say it aloud, reminding myself to be mindful of my heritage and position in Nuafri society. Young Nuafri are expected to find balance by observing, and to incorporate the lessons learned in our smooth cities, but also from the roots of the gnarliest trees outside them. We must walk both sides of the street, the roughest and smoothest forest paths. My ophanti allow me to do both, even though some members of the Shanta Order wait for me to outgrow them.

They must wait a little while yet, which, as Akalie knows, is as long as the root of a pomark tree.

To locate Tifundu I need help, so hold out my hand until Akalie lands there, flattening her wings back and turning her bulbous eye on me as we study each other. Her body mixes

"Really?" Wendu Weike snaps his finger and thumb at Akalie, releasing the latent energy in his palm pads. She spins away as if bludgeoned with the blunt end of a spear. "That," he says, as I gasp at Akalie's dizzying flight to recovery, "is why you must leave the ophanti. Let a new acolyte pick up the pieces. You are too close. You lose sight of the greater work of the Order. We are not destined to sweep the streets of undesirables, only to learn from them. Our fate – *yours*, when you regain your senses – is to tease at the threads of existence, and to weave them in such a fashion that we can make string, cord, and rope, drawing the secrets of the universe to us, as we pull hand over hand," he mimics the action, something I have seen him do many, many times, "until we find the centre and conceive our place in the whole. That is your purpose, Afua Toure."

It is his favourite speech, and one we are expected to swallow every time. But he knows nothing. If he truly grasped those threads then he wouldn't seduce young acolytes on a forest walk, where the only cord he is interested in is the one she wears as a belt around her waist. Tied loosely, I see, and I am pretty sure it is because he seized it, pulling it hand over hand ...

"Afua Toure? Are you listening to me?"

"Yea, Wendu Weike."

Akalie is recovered, and I can look at Wendu now.

"Good," he says. "Now, if you release your Dooga, you can walk with Oba and myself back to the Order. We are to gather before nightfall, ready for ninth day recension."

"I can't walk with you," I say, wondering how Mez would react if I revealed what Wendu Weike had been doing? "I am looking for Tifundu."

"Let me guess. He is one of your ophanti saplings."

"And missing, since yesterday."

"Then he is yesterday's problem. Afua Toure, you must let them go. You are a promising acolyte, far more intelligent than Oba."

Oba's left eye twitches at what Wendu Weike has just said. I experience a similar surge of irritation, but there is little we can say or do about it. The Shanta Order is steeped in tradition.

Akalie settles into a hover above my left shoulder. The brush of air from her wings fans my resistance. If nothing else, thoughts of me will occupy Wendu Weike all the way back to the city, sparing Oba from any more of his selfish intentions.

"Tifundu is missing," I say. "I will find him, and then I will return for recension."

"You will sit in the outer circle if you do," Wendu Weike snarls, as if he is a mating Kchak.

"So be it," I reply.

Akalie has emitted baby gas – potent enough that even Wendu Weike coughs in the Dooga cloud, and Oba giggles. Softly and respectfully, yes, but aloud – and that is the difference.

Akalie transitions into forward flight just as I notice Wendu Weike's fists are clenched. Two fast strides put me between him and Akalie as he prepares to cast a pulse from his palm. I remember the day I received my palm pads. My guardian – on a brief period of leave from the bridge of the Nuafri cruiser Lalasalama – taught me to catch pulses on the rooftop of our sky tower. Gentle oscillations, barely tickling my palms as I caught them.

Wendu Weike's pulse crackles and spits through the air as he hurls it at Akalie.

I think of her fat belly, and the six baby Dooga wriggling inside her. Does she anticipate the danger? Does she have a chemical anaesthetic she can flood through her body to protect them?

She doesn't have to.

My guardian taught me well, and I catch Wendu Weike's pulse, gasping in pain as I do so, before absorbing his evil energy with a grimace.

"Fly high, Akalie," I say as she flashes past my cheek to attack.

My right hand burns red, and the last splash of litrus paint crisps from my fingers. Oba, my witness, glares at Wendu Weike. I doubt he will talk about me on his return. If Oba is smart – and I know she is – she will tuck this one away, but not so far that Wendu Weike thinks she has forgotten the day he burned an acolyte's hand.

"I will find Tifundu," I state, hiding the searing pain as I depart.

Yes, I will find him. But first I must locate an abrashik root, *a'brashika* meaning "weeps medicine when cut". Even the thought of spreading its juice is like nectar. And I must not dally, or my palm will be scarred for life. I don't want to be reminded of Wendu Weike every time I clench my fist.

The day is turning, and in the dense forest beneath the cathedral trees and thick canopies, I need light to find an abrashik root. Wendu Weike's bolt fried my palm pads, but I still have Jatta's kirant spores, and I whip up a quick batch of paint, holding up

My breath is still held as it arches its spine, splaying its quills which ripple pink through yellow before fading back to earthy browns and iridescent greens.

I bunch my good fist and feel the energy weave into a steady stream, like blistering yarn wrapped around my fingers.

The ears of the Kchak are my second clue, since they were erect when it was startled, but are now flat as the spikes on its back bristle up.

I count the beats of my pulse as the palm pad charges, and stand slowly, without the threat of sudden movement, hoping it will want to avoid a confrontation.

The Kchak retreats, head low.

Oh, I know the mantra. All children learn it. "Before it strikes, the Kchak steps back."

The question was no longer: would the creature chase me?

No. The question became: how accurate were Kchak at shooting those deadly barbs?

I throw myself to the side at the same moment that it fires with kcha-kcha-kcha sounds, and I roll back to a kneeling position even as the barbs thunk into thick trunks by my side. I may only have seconds, so aim with my hand and flex as I yell, so that the powerful charge bursts into life. I see with my mind's eye the Kchak receiving the energy blast on its side with the smell of charred hair and blistered cells as the Kchak leaps away, surging into the undergrowth.

Except that doesn't happen. Instead, my pulse sends up clouds of dry earth that crackle before us. The damage to its partner pad must have limited its storage capacity, and the result is certainly not the startling effect I'd hoped for. Even the Kchak squints disdainfully at the barely displaced soil.

Palm pads are meant to be less a weapon than a deterrent, since it is bad luck to hurt wildlife, and worse to kill it. But mine have failed on both fronts.

The mist above the Kchak parts in a tight V as a Dooga buzzes a finger's width above the triangular head. The insect spins and dips low, barrelling back towards the Kchak before snapping into a right angle a split second before impact. The Kchak stalls on the path, tilting its head as it searches for the Dooga.

Not just *any* Dooga. Akalie's paint glows with the kirant of hope.

My heart races and I try to restore charge, whilst praying the palm pad already has some unused capacity, that it had stored more than it released. I move in a fast squat while the Kchak snaps at the air with its oversized teeth while Akalie performs another run past its head, swooping just out of a collision course. The Kchak stutters to one side, twisting, presenting the softer side of its flank to me as Akalie flies tight circles above the Kchak's head.

I jog closer to the beast, splaying my fingers.

"Fly high, Akalie" I shout, just before the pulse is released.

This time it does shock the Kchak, at least slightly. I don't hang around to see the effect but sprint away, leaping knobbly roots and undergrowth, ducking under low branches. The flicker-flack of wings accompanies me, my brave Dooga swishing through gaps in the foliage at my side.

I keep my breath regular and avoid any yells when I scrape bare knees, or thorns tear at my skin and rip the hem of my green-gold tunic. Even when racing through the forest we are trained to do so as quietly as possible, to avoid the perils of making *prey noises*. The sound of a wounded animal could draw further predators out of the trees, out of the roots, even out of the earth itself.

There might be a grace to my movements, but it does not last long enough. I trip over a thin root as it hooks around my ankle. A moment later I am slapped onto the ground, eating dirt and needles as my lips bruise on the packed earth. The fall thumps the air out of my lungs, and it takes many counts before I catch my breath again.

It is a chance to check for pursuit, flicking my gaze along the path I'd created as the foetid smell of meat and shit fills my nose.

I tremble when I see that thick beast on stubby legs lumbering after me, its back covered in quills like a phalanx of missiles on a Nuafri cruiser. The Kchak smashes saplings out of the way, tears through vines and knotted weed.

It must be hungry. Or very angry.

Probably both.

I am on my feet and running again, though tumbling and bumping might be a more accurate description. Silence is less of a goal than speed, now. With enough of a head start I could climb, up through the branches and out of the Kchak's way. If it was a netwood tree I could perhaps hook into the nuon biochannels and signal for help. Even if my message has to cross multiple nodes of PSV data networks, help would come before long.

The ground slopes upwards, and unfortunately the geological disturbances that affect this region lead to broken areas of bare rock rather than tree cover. Before long I am exposed in sunlight half the time, with sparse vegetation to hide me.

Akalie buzzes ahead, spiralling. When I ignore her as a distraction she swoops over and nips me before returning to the dip where her strange swirls began. I detour, standing on the rim of crumbly yellow lemstone, and see what she indicates.

A gap in the rock. A thin, black crack squeezed between two slabs of ruin.

Of course. This region, as is fairly common for Nuafri, has a subsurface of porous saltstone. It forms natural tunnels, many of which we use as transport networks beneath cities. And, in geologically unstable zones, it is not unusual for the ground to collapse, revealing sinkholes beneath the land.

I scuttle my way down the gritty scree, coming to a halt by the dark passage into the earth.

Akalie never ceases to amaze me. She had worked out I needed somewhere to hide, and she found this, which … no. I kneel and examine some damp earth by the crack.

A small footprint. About the size of Tifundu's.

Perhaps she wasn't looking for an escape, but indicating a trace she'd followed.

I look for other signs. Unfortunately, much of the rocky surface here is too hard and dry to leave marks, but I do find more footprints. The direction is clear: into the hole. And the spacing between each, combined with the deeply imprinted toes, suggests running. Further, sharp contours, where edges have yet to collapse into the indentations, imply recent creation.

So if it was Tifundu, he might have been fleeing a creature, just as I was. That makes sense if this area is currently the territory of a mating Kchak pair.

My left palm dries in the warm forest air, while I try to ignore the pain returning in my right. It is too soon to paint my palm with abrashik juice again, no matter how much I would like to. I peer into the gap, but the daylight does not reach far before it is overpowered by darkness.

However, Akalie's litrus glow reflects off the stone. A child would not venture far, and might be drawn to light. Ideas swirl within me.

Yes, I have seen this kind of uncharted tunnel before, many times on my meditation walks, and would never normally enter alone. What sensible person would? It is an ideal lair for some of the stranger, rarer, more deadly Nuafri wildlife. But where once I saw *peril*, now I look with Tifundu's eyes and see *shelter*. And if Tifundu squeezed into it, then with a little squirming I can do likewise.

The same gene I suffer when resisting is also my *curious* and *courageous* gene. It is my Chromosomal Lifeprint. Therefore it is natural that I am curious, but I will need all my courage to slither into the darkness, especially now my palm pads are defunct. We Nuafri are taught to tune into our surroundings. Our technology has furthered the integration of the forest, the atmosphere, the planet. Receptors in my skin breathe forest spores, examining them for mysteries and messages from Nuafri. And yet, as I kneel hesitantly in front of the gap, my receptors are clogged as if *I* am clogged. The blackness is heady and solemn.

The eleventh Shanta precept is the duty to investigate that which scares us. *Flee not the night; you learn nothing from your back, for it is eyeless.*

I would be a fool to enter for no good reason. To risk my life in such a way.

But I will do it for Tifundu.

And then Akalie is at my ear, purging soft pulses of baby gas as she catches breath from her weighted flight. I wrinkle my nose, but her close presence and juddery movements might indicate an approaching threat. If so, I just hope it comes from behind, not ahead.

“Akalie,” I whisper. “Fly low.”

I urge her into the black with a nod. She is Dooga, but we are bound to one another. Straining to see her light as she slips into the space between the two ruined walls, I follow.

The Discovery

Inside, the crack is narrow at first. Grit falls into my eyes as I squirm and shunt my shoulders along. What I do with care could also be accomplished with strength, and a lumbering, broad-shouldered Kchak would soon tear its way in. I try not to dwell on those images while I am forced to crawl.

As I shuggle along I am enveloped by a blister of something alternately cold and hot, as if the air cannot decide what it wishes. I shiver when the hairs rise on my naked arms, but as the air turns from icy to steamy my skin is beaded with sweat. And so it cycles through temperatures, stopping short of maximums and minimums, as if to say *come, continue. It will be no better, no worse. Come, Afua.*

It knows my name.

Something knows my name.

Perhaps Tifundu called for me in fright, when the black surrounded him, and he was lost. If it is so, and it is the echo of his fear, then I might choose to be happy about that, knowing that in his time of terror, my ophanti needed me.

No sign of Akalie. No sparkle of kirant yellow in the darkness, during the moments when I can blink grains and web out of my eyes. She has gone ahead, brave despite her size. And yet, her trail is clear, and I draw strength from the bubbles of baby gas she spills in her wake. I follow them, sniff for them, rolling my shoulders and hips like a ssanju worm, digging my elbows into the earthy floor like Dooga teeth, pulling myself deeper.

And before long the fissure opens up again. I crawl until I can crouch, then walk as soon as I am able. The roof slopes upwards, while the floor goes down. A cave in the earth.

I am rubbing my eyes clear of debris (not with huge success, since my hands are covered in dirt) when another burst of gas indicates Akalie is close. Her wings flutter loose strands of my hair, tickling my cheeks, and again she gives me strength. She flies above my head, and I reach for her, stretching until the tips of my fingers scrape the roof of the cave. The air is cool and damp at the top, but warmer, sweatier, around my hips, my knees, before heating my bare feet to the degree that they will likely blister.

"The temperature shift doesn't make any sense, Akalie."

She releases more gas, which may mean she agrees, or perhaps her babies want out and a sudden pain stabs in my chest that I have deprived her of nesting. No green leaves exist inside the cave, just scorching floor angling down and away into the unknown.

Akalie recovers her yellow sparkle in the warm, lower layers, and I am grateful for her company. She doesn't provide enough light to see far, but that is fine. I have my methods, and on the undamaged palm I activate my fingerlights modification. The threads that run under the skin, one down each finger, all end in a subcutaneous biopatch powered by the palm pad. My fingertips emit slender white beams, and I squat to examine the earthy coating to the rough rock ahead of me.

Yes, shadows indicating depth, prints. A child came this way, and continued, its steps much closer together now and indicating careful tread in the darkness. A Nuafri child would not possess the palm pads and their associated tools, such as fingerlights.

And if they moved so slowly and cautiously, then there is a good chance I will catch up, and recover the sapling, and bring it back into the light where it can grow.

The cave is luckily not a widely branching network, like the Sulstar saltstone labyrinth. This is much more of a split in the earth, like a piece of bluewood cleaved by an axe, only on the scale of tremendous natural forces. And I have been following it for some time when I hear strange sounds echoing faintly.

I stop to listen, head tilted. It requires effort to filter out the rushing in my ears, the shift of falling earth, the trickle of water. At first I worry that it might be geological activity. Tremors shake my heels, perhaps aftershocks from the energy that created this fissure in the first place. This cavity in the earth might well become a tomb if the ground twists again, hiding what was revealed. A death by suffocation or crushing was not part of my plan this ninth day.

Then I wonder if the sound is an echoing snarl, some chesty, guttural warning. Just like a Kchak might emit when it finds a prey trail.

I apply pressure to the correct points of my adductor pollicis muscle on my left hand, and the fingerlights turn off. Although Kchak have many senses, it would be stupid to reveal myself visually from a distance. Their eyes are sensitive to even a few photons of light which ricochet between surfaces. My best hope is that it loses interest before coming into close proximity.

"Fly high, Akalie," I say. Then, after a moment, even though the concepts might be too advanced for her to understand: "But be careful of your wings on the roof."

Up she goes, her light diminishing in the cooler air up there. It is the best I can do to reduce our visual traces. Akalie's echo location will help her avoid obstacles. A Dooga's single compound eye is never the best instrument for depth perception.

And onwards I move, though this time on hands and knees, so as to reduce my chances of slipping or tripping on the uneven, often slick surface. Sharp flints stab my skin and sweat drips in my eyes as I crawl within the strangely heated layer. Breathing does not come easy.

It's a relief when I enter a pocket of frigid air, probably caused by the complex shifting of currents in conjunction with irregular, rocky outcrops.

The relief soon fades when I realise the chill comes from the hole in front of me into which my arm falls, followed immediately after by the rest of my body.

I am attacked by brambles, the thorns catch at my hair, wanting to tear out my roots to nourish their own ... and I continue to wake, groggy, sore. The sensation wasn't a dream but something else. Spindly legs scratch me, and my horror of giant piznids seizes me before I correctly identify the sensations.

A Dooga's claws caught in my hair, the insect's wings buzzing and slapping me.

I taste blood in my mouth. My tongue prods around. No broken teeth, just a bite out of my cheek. And the pain in my limbs seems to be from bruising rather than breaking. My head aches, like my brain's become too big for the skull. But I'm alive, and piecing myself together, thought by thought.

"It's okay, Akalie." I sit up carefully while she extricates herself from the knots she had been tugging to wake me. "I'm okay."

Despite the risks, I activate fingerlights. The beams are weak until I take deep breaths and clench my fist a number of times in the same pattern as my heart. Then they strengthen and I can try to work out where I am.

Far above is the hole I fell down. I was lucky not to strike rock, but instead landed on the residues that have accrued over time. Soil, leaves, dirt and gravel, it has all slipped and gathered in the mound under my bottom, absorbing the worst of the impact. My upward inspection is rewarded with a shushing drizzle of sandy dust in my face, making me cough and blink.

"By the Spirit's shadow," I splutter.

"Afua," a querulous voice nearby says. The light beams brighten as my heart leaps in panic at the thought of roho ghosts, and the discovery that I wasn't alone in darkness.

I point my fingers anyway, expecting the worst, but rewarded with the best: Tifundu, crouching nearby. Akalie flies a little higher, and her soft light reveals the streaks on his muddy face.

"Yes, it's me. It's Afua. I have found you my little restless one."

"You found me," he says, before bursting into tears.

We hug until he calms, and despite the pains, I smile at the familiar scent and sounds of my ophanti. And, at the same time, I sniff for Kchak, and listen for bass grunts from above.

"You're cut," he says, once his eyes have adjusted to the light of my fingers and Akalie after so long in the darkness.

"I have some abrashik. What about you, Tifundu? Are you hurt?"

"'Sokay now. Did you take the fourth root?" he asks. "You're not meant to cut the first you find." His pupils are large, as if he must be vigilant, as if he must see everything at once.

"That's right, Tifundu. And I followed the rules. But sometimes, when we are hurt, it's okay to make exceptions. That is worth remembering."

I use my knife to peel more of the abrashik skin and apply it to my palm, and a few cuts on Tifundu. He takes pleasure in patting some around my own lacerations, and soon the plant works its magic, diminishing pain in a cooling numbness.

The root is finished, so I slip my knife into the sheath on my belt and stand. Akalie hovers above my shoulder as Tifundu and I gaze upwards at the rough overhang that dumped us both down here.

There is no chance of climbing it, or even boosting each other. Too many overhangs that look far too crumbly to take our weight, with the ceiling hole some distance from the nearest wall.

I take Tifundu's hand.

"We'll find another way out," I say.

Akalie buzzes close by, and all the while my palm grows moist with ophanti sweat.

But it is not just Tifundu who sweats.

I have heard the sounds of pursuit. The Kchak is still there. I did not want to scare Tifundu, but decided it was better if he knew the danger we faced, and prepared for it. His head twitches while we walk, and I imagine the tips of his ears prickling as he listens, nostrils flaring as he sniffs, skin tingling as he feels for danger.

There are more pockets of heat. Sweat runs down his brow to splash on thick eyelashes, and then onto his lips. He licks them away, presses tiny teeth into his bottom lip. Tifundu was the brashest of all the ophanti and his fear worries me beyond the concern I would normally show the restless ones.

"You have been so brave," I say, squeezing his hand.

"I wasn't scared," he tells me, in an almost-convincing manner. "It was just very dark. And there were funny noises in these tunnels, especially from the deeper roads ... routes ... rooms. Whatever."

"What kind of noises?"

"I don't know. Echoes, and clicking, and humming like an engine, and footsteps, and ... well, lots."

Some created by a vivid imagination, no doubt.

My own is also nagging at me. This lower level of cave is more regular than that above. Earth and exposed rock give way to flatter surfaces, some stained with residue, or oxidised minerals. I kneel and brush soil to the side, to find a shale-like subsurface which is pitted, and yet not quite like rock.

That sends me to the left wall of this passage. On sweeping away the grime and wiry roots I find more of the same. Corroded, greys and browns.

Akalie returns to my side, and I blink in her light as she settles on my shoulder.

"I know what this is, and it's not a cave."

I think Tifundu suspected it too, although he couldn't put a name to it like I can.

"This is the wreck of a spaceship," I whisper, cupping my hand above Akalie to feel the tickle of her wing tips on my palm.

Sometimes ancient wreckages are discovered. They are treated with reverence, and the ruins may become places of meditation, or archaeological curiosity. If discovered by an outcast and kept secret it can be adopted as a camp, with scavenged ship parts sold to the cities for as long as the source can be kept hidden. Tectonic shifts are often the cause of the unearthings. I never imagined I might come upon one of their resting places.

In my mind I remove some of the earth and stone, rebuild surfaces, to try and get a feel for the geographies of this location with fresh eyes. Understanding its original shape and function may offer opportunities.

The path is not wide enough to be a main corridor. I think it is a service conduit, which means I must be somewhere along the hull. I strain my brain to remember anything about spaceship layouts, but it is muddled. Snippets of chapter disc information always seemed so much more remote than the life and forest around me, so that the studies were not retained. And ancient craft were obviously different from our sleek Arboreus warships. Still, I shift my gaze upwards as we walk. Perhaps more a superstition than a suspicion.

A thick cluster of milky roots form a tangle up high. But this is reachable. I hook my foot into a rusty hole, careful of the jagged edges, and raise myself so I can try and separate the root tendrils for a better look.

Yes. Behind them is a hole. And when I stick my head in, I see a dirty metallic tunnel running off in both directions. Some kind of broken ventilation duct.

Another boon when I face the upward-sloping direction and inhale deeply. Beneath the damp and rich earth smell is a delicate scent of sap, surface leaves. Even a tickle on the fine hairs of my face, as if air is shifted by a breeze. I disable my fingerlights for a minute and let my eyes adjust. It might be imagination, but I think there is the faintest trace of light in the distance.

That is hope.

Unfortunately, the duct is far too small for my own body.

I lower myself back to the gritty slope below, and am about to explain all this to Tifundu when a heavy thud echoes from the way we came. It sounds like a creature leaping down a hole, on the trail of prey. I don't need my imagination to tell me that the Kchak is not far behind, blocking any hope of retreat.

"Listen carefully, Tifundu." I kneel so I am at his height. "There's a crawlspace up there which should be a snug fit for you, my little ssanju worm. It may lead upwards to the surface, probably the ground has been split in a number of fractures. You must crawl up there, find a way out."

"I won't leave you!" he says. "We need to look out for each other! You tell us, 'Pairing is safer when facing danger'."

"I do say that, but all rules require exceptions. To save me, you have to do this, because once you are out it is your responsibility to go and find help. And that's how you pair with me, by actions that save me, see? The end result is the same."

"I can't reach it like you."

"I know. But remember the frogym flip we all practised, where a kid can help a partner reach high branches in the forest?"

"So we can scuttle along and get the high fruit."

"Exactly. We'll do that."

I brace my back to the wall, cup my hands, and provide him with the ladder he needs. Tifundu scrambles up, light as a hedge rat, only knocking my head once with a misplaced elbow. Then I stand, using arm strength to fling him up where he catches the edge and manages to gain a secure position.

"It's dark in there," he says.

"I've already thought of that," I reassure him. "Akalie – you fly high. Lead him out so he can see. And do *not* return: once you reach the outside, go and nest and give birth to your babies. You are released."

I find the lack of noise from behind to be more worrying than if the Kchak lumbered in its normal manner. It means the creature knows it is close to me, and is adopting stealth. It also means I have no idea whether it is a minute away, or about to leap from the darkness, and maul me in the unpleasantly agonising way they are known for. Kchak claws can separate tendon from bone with great finesse.

"Go!" I urge.

Akalie buzzes up the tunnel ahead of Tifundu, and he begins his wriggly ascent after her. But even when he is out of sight I can hear the muffled thumps of his passage. So would a predator. And maybe the Kchak can climb or leap enough to swat at the thin metal that holds the boy.

Nothing else for it. I will have to be the more tempting target.

"Hey! Over here! Come find me!" I call into the blackness behind, whilst reactivating my fingerlights. The glow from my hand will make me visible. It also means I will have to move quicker, and pray that this is not a dead end.

I sweat as I run away, hooting and hollering, and this time the sweat isn't due to a hot pocket of air. My life is in play, and I entreat that today is *not* a good day to die.

Native Fauna: A Lecture

The songs of Nuafri's Divade singers are not just entertainment. They are oral history, parables, myths, practical guidance, folklore, and biological understanding.

And many of them concern the reptile-resembling Kchak. It's an N1 organism that fascinates humans as much as it terrifies children when it appears in stories warning them to behave lest they end up in said beast's belly.

If you ask anyone in the Tumani system what makes the Kchak unique, you will hear many different answers. But one of the most common facts relates to the creature's barbed quills. Just like this one, I hold up before you.

Yes, please pass it on after examination. Don't worry, it has been sterilised. Pay attention to the tiny hooks behind the tip, which will catch on any clothing. Also note that the barb is as long as an arm, as thick as an index finger, and as sharp as the knives Nuafri residents used to cut abrashik creepers.

Just three barbs to the chest is fatal. They will pierce sternums, clavicles and ribs as easily as paper.

Kchak are solitary beings, unless denning. The female is plagued during the early period of denning by the male's repeated attempts to mount her. The male is either stupid, horny, or both. Please settle down. Either way, this period is the most active of the Kchak's life. It is certainly the best time to observe them.

Except, that is sometimes easier said than done. Kchak alter their skin pigmentation to match their surroundings – for defence *and* offence. But they are slow. It's unlikely a Kchak will *chase* its prey. It favours surprising its quarry. It is an opportunist. But they will track. With their highly evolved senses, tracking is possible even in complete darkness. And they can be persistent. Folk songs suggest the Kchak has *endless* patience.

When active – such as mating time – the male Kchak struggles to maintain an even pigmentation. In fact, the skin appears to ripple. During this time, the beast thinks of one thing only. Not unlike many of you, I'm sure.

Further research is needed, and efforts are underway to raise Kchak in captivity. Obviously, their acquisition has to be done via clandestine means, as the Nuafri won't allow trade in native fauna, or removal from their habitats. To date, our breeding efforts have been unsuccessful. It seems the Kchak have a suicide switch, relating to their *do or die* approach to life. In the event they are captured, and escape appears impossible, these beasts would rather die than suffer a life of captivity. Kchak merits – if you choose to see them as such – could be transferred to our own people. In this particular line of work, intelligence officers should adopt the Kchak's approach to life.

Of course, the Kchak has one more weapon – a *secret* weapon even the Kchak is unaware of. The Kchak is a reservoir for the

Idiramoti virus – particularly virulent, and dormant inside the Kchak's blood. No, you are safe handling that quill. The quills are thick, as you've seen, and propelled with such force they will skewer and maim anything unfortunate enough to be struck by them. The Kchak doesn't need poison. The Idiramoti relies on a vector to transfer it from the reservoir to a host.

There are many good reasons why the Derago, with its single eye and scratchy hair-like claws, is on the Nuafri flag. Mimicry, for one, is a Nuafri virtue – in business, science, and warfare. Imagine if we, like the Derago, could fool our enemy with imitation. If we could look like them, sound like them ... well, that's for tomorrow's lecture. But the point for today: the Derago's size is legendary, not because it is huge ... but *because it is tiny.* Much smaller than the semi-domesticated Dooga it somewhat resembles.

The Derago, too, can alter its pigmentation. We believe this is the reason the Idiramoti virus can exist in both the Kchak and the Derago, without killing them, or making them sick. Unfortunately, the virus has a different effect on its human host. We'll be covering the results of our experiments in the near future. Potentially agonising for the victim, but for the observer ... well, you'll see.

Which brings me to the conclusion of this lecture. To be an effective Agent, one must master the following skills. *Observation. Patience. Mimicry.*

And, it helps to have a sense of humour.

The Descent

The tickle of excitement from action soon catches in my throat as I search my memory for anything and everything I know about old spaceships. I can hardly see a few lengths ahead, let alone any detail or a clear delineation of where the ruined ship frame ends, and rock begins. And yet, I must be on an outer surface, even if the ship was inverted or crashed on its side. And that means to go further in, is to go down.

I pause for a moment to examine the floor of the cave. My nail taps against something sturdy, something metal. I thump it. Hollow. Sweeping leaves away reveals metal grilles, perhaps where cables and pipes ran beneath, but now thick with soil and scree.

It is hard to be sure, but I think this really was flooring, not a ceiling cover. And my memory pulls something up about corridors having hatches. Or maybe I'm getting mixed up with modern ships.

I move slower, pushing aside debris every now and again. Eyes focus down, while ears focus back for any sound of pursuit. Yes, it's a shame I don't have the sensitive and motile pointy ears some types of high-canopy monkeys possess.

Eventually the reward comes while dipping my fingers into the earth and feeling around. My nails scratch against a hinge. I trace the thin gap around the hatch until a handle is revealed. Corroded and rusty.

I wish I had worn my expedition outfit today. Its folded hem contains pouches of useful gels, such as antiseptics, coagulants, and antivenoms. If only I'd known this ninth day would break the pattern of laughter and company. Some of the gels would have doubled as lubricants. Then I remember the litrus nut. Luckily the pocket has not been torn in my sprint through the tangled forest. I remove it and scoop out some of the slimy interior, massaging it into the handle and hinges liberally. Then I apply as much effort as I can. At first nothing happens except the risk of bursting the blood vessels in my eyes, so that everything is stars; but then it begins to turn, and that perhaps breaks the hold. Soon it is in the open position and I can heave it up. I lift the crackling hatch, shivering with excitement and no small amount of trepidation.

Air is sucked into my face from below. Stale and cold, like a crypt. Undisturbed for centuries, perhaps. But at least that means I won't be dropping into a Kchak den.

Still, even when I shine my fingerlights down, I can't be sure how high the corridor beneath is. I may be seeing a hint of metal, or that could be some layer of mist or weird faint reflection. If I drop down more than a few lengths I will break myself and live the last hours of life alone inside a derelict spaceship. I will become a part of Nuafri history, literally, my body exhumed and exhibited, if it is ever found.

The gulf below me is blacker than the original cave entrance.

Then I hear the noise. Like the rusty hinges, guttural. I don't think I knocked the hatch as I moved around. Which means it must be the Kchak, getting closer.

That decides things for me. I have no chance fighting a Kchak with my small blade. So I grasp the sides of the hatch, wincing as I rediscover pain in my right palm. Strangely, my left also tingles, as if my skin receptors have come unclogged, or someone has prised them open with the tip of a knife.

Something wants to get inside me, to seep through my pores and to *share* things.

Wondrous things.

I drop.

Air rushes past.

I brace myself for impact and it comes soon, so that I land in a crouch but it is still bone-jarring. Tomorrow I will be all bruises and moans.

If I survive.

This wide throughway is obviously derelict and decaying, running with damp rivulets, creaking and rusty, but it is still in better condition than the area above. Here, you immediately *know* this is the ruins of a craft.

And that doesn't help me much. Down here there is unlikely to be another route to the surface. My goal is not to escape, but to hide and hope Tifundu alerts someone, so a track-and-rescue team is sent. And for that reason, I can't go too far from the entrance, especially if seismic activity here might limit their search. I need to be ready to reveal myself.

And so, I need guidance.

I follow the passage in the direction I face, because the air there smells fresher. Though "fresh" is relative down here – it is all dampness, corrosion, and a nasty undertone of who-knows-what.

Eventually a junction reveals itself. Faint and indefinable sounds echo back and forth between the passageways. But I don't intend to wander randomly. In the every-direction of the forest we look for signs, to reveal what really exists. And I hope there will be signs here, too, for the people of the past. Junctions mean options, and many people like to be guided. So I scan the walls with my fingerlights, pulsing my palms to keep them charged, trying to identify any grime-covered detail that could be a sign.

I almost miss it at first. Beneath a cluster of lumps that remind me of shells and which I assume are just a mouldy growth of some kind, I catch a hint of orange near the ceiling. Too high to reach. But there are rails attached to the walls – gravity rails? I pull myself up and balance on one, tight against the wall. This enables me to brush aside the crusty shells. They give up their hold and fall with a dessicated crinkle, like a long-dead snail when you pull it from its resting place. I scratch away at the residue with my fingernail, until I can make out at least part of the faded orange directional signage below.

There seem to be words, but I can't make them out, due to the deterioration, and ancient dialect. Perhaps that word means tube? A transportation tube or shuttle, as used for transit around a large craft? If so, that's not where I want to go. Dark tunnels are the perfect hunting ground for Kchak.

Another direction has blue symbols I recognise, even if the words are strange – an image of a bed stacked on top of another, like tree hammocks in the Sulstar suburbs. Private chambers for these ship people. The perfect place for concealment.

I head in that direction, occasionally glimpsing emergency flashes of blue on the wall that confirm I am going the correct way.

The weird red-shell growths coat the walls and floor in some places, and I cannot avoid treading on them. They crunch unpleasantly under my bare feet; sharp, but not enough to cut me.

The Kchak's claws and teeth would not be so kind.

This ship is a warren of corridors. It might take days to walk it all, passing between areas of heat and ice from one end to the other. I stop in a pocket of cool air to catch my breath, purging hot staleness from my lungs, before continuing. There is a junction ahead, and I slow on my approach, curious that this section of the ship appears undamaged. I would know for sure if the ship's illumination worked, but all I have is the faint yellow beams of fingerlights.

The age-worn sign shows me I have reached the area I sought. An accommodation zone, with a Kchak-proof metal door. Which would be a cause for joy if I could enter easily. Unfortunately, the heavy doors are closed, and I cannot find any rope loop or handle with which to pull it open.

Closer examination reveals a security pad to the side, partly hidden by the encrustation of dull cherry shells. I pick enough away to make space for my hand and press my palm against the smooth glass, but nothing happens. This kind of door needs power, but the ship died long ago, and it has no chance of being resurrected.

Or does it?

I pump my fist in time with my heart, feeling for each beat of life, letting the charge grow. When I place my palm this time and release the energy something strange happens. The scanner prickles my palm in recognition and the shells glow a ruby red, casting a veil of bloody light over the wall. And at first I think that is all, a minor mystery, until pained groans shake the ground beneath me, and the door moves with the stiffness of ancient bones in a Filiate elder.

Creaky, but movement nonetheless, wheezing its way onwards as the door lumbers to my right, sliding into a recess in the bulkhead. Then it shudders to a halt, dead again. It is no matter. I squeeze into the gap between the red shell lights to enter the chamber beyond.

It is not some small bedroom, but a large enclosure with a domed ceiling. Around the edge are beds in pairs, one on top of another. Small privacy screens separate one section from the next. I wonder if there are other exits, across the room in the darkness.

Not full darkness. Red light shimmers from behind one screen. Although my instincts wriggle in warning, I am curious, so I shuffle closer in silence and peer around the edge.

It is a body. On the lower bunk. Except, not a full body, because time has passed and all that remains is a crumbly skeleton dressed in the rags of a uniform. Among the bones are more of the scarlet shells. Many of them are open, and it's from them that the red light emits, in a slow pulse like breathing as it brightens and dims. They have made their home in the corpse.

The clothing is too tattered to read the name badge, since it was sewn on in fabric. But on each side of the beds are big lockers, and one of them has a corroded metal plate slipped in for identification. It may be the person's name.

Tlalli, M.

Were they a man or a woman? Or something else? When we become skeletons the question fades away. But I feel a hint of identification, could imagine myself living in such quarters, surrounded by metal and plastic. Whoever made this bed and locker their temporary home was untidy. Clothes are piled in heaps on the cold, cross-hatched metal floor. A basin below a dirt-flecked mirror is strewn with grooming articles. Wrappers and empty containers layer themselves in gravity drifts in the corners where the screens jut out. It reminds me of attempts to disguise the squareness of it all – breaking the lines of order can be an act of resistance.

Yes, I would have lived like this.

"I'm sorry you died," I tell the old bones.

I smear the mirror with a palm to see myself, wide-eyed, looking more like something from a horror story than the self I recognise. A story told by ophanti to scare each other around a fire.

The thought makes me smile, and I sit at the end of the bed to rest a moment, though being careful not to disturb the bones and their weird, glowing infestation.

They do say that if you can smile on a bad day, then good will come your way.

As I shine my fingerlights around I realise some of the lockers are set apart from the rest. Larger, with a convex door implying something big is stored inside, as if it bulges to escape. Once I have recovered some energy I get up to examine it. The door is stiff, but the horizontal handle is long and gives me good leverage as I tug. Finally a catch is released and the door squeaks open like a monkey's call.

The tall monster inside makes me gasp and flinch back from the thick arms before I can be grabbed, and I am ready to run but it does not move. Its faceplate reflects my lights with a blankness akin to meditation.

And still, there is not a twitch.

Then thoughts connect, and I place its appearance in lessons I once received. Tutors had suggested knowledge of space suit technology was like understanding Nuafri sentence structure – without the basics, neither could be used. I remember protesting that I was unlikely to ever need a Barka Shieldsuit in the forest.

Well, this is no Barka, but is likely some more primitive form of EVA suit. Closer examination shows that it is carapace exo-armour clamped around a simple fabric shell, with attached mobility packs and tool pockets. Life support is no doubt integral, as would be the suit interface.

Protection from hostile environments. Armour that can absorb impact.

However, when I try to bend the suit's arm I find it is locked solidly in place. No doubt it is a powered item, and requires activation as well as an energy source. I play around with a control panel on the forearm, trying to get some sign of life. There is no response, even when I add a gentle palm pad of energy that shouldn't fry anything.

That is frustrating, but all situations can offer possibilities to those who truly see. With time and a spindle of biothreads I could maybe repair it fully. Even without those, I may separate some parts out and gain a bit of armour for protection against scratches and bumps. I seize a wrist gauntlet and twist, rewarded with the click of a disengaging lock, when the Kchak arrives.

It is my fault for lingering too long, enabling it to track me, to hear my sounds. But I am so tired, I needed this rest.

The Kchak suffers no fatigue. Even though the door's gap is too narrow for its three-hundred-plus kilogram bulk, it has got most of its head through and now wriggles, pushing its bunched-up shoulder muscles. Claws gouge metal flooring for traction, widening the gap fraction by fraction despite the door's stiffness. It is said the Kchak can generate almost a Tuu of forward force, and a rusty door will not resist that for long.

I race in the opposite direction, discovering an exit that lets me get further from the ferocious, frustrated snarling. More of the red shells grow in the dampest regions of the corridor, and these also glow with wavering, bloody light. But it lets me see more easily, which in turn lets me run down this tilted passage. The pinprick lights of the embedded glow-shells seem to awake ahead of me, until the deck is alight with flash striping. It leads me along to unknown depths.

The Truth

The walls sparkle as I run, shells opening and closing, blinking like pincer bulbs. These tiny eyes lead my way as do safety lights in the corridor of a Nuafri public building. I follow them deeper, not risking a pause to catch my breath as the path steepens.

Although my way forward is lit, one after another the shells close behind me, turning off their beady lights with soft claps. They may just be reacting to motion, or – one of my silly thoughts – they may be guiding me, then hiding me from what follows. Which would make them allies, in a way.

Either that, or just another predator, using lazy guile in place of energetic pursuit.

My flight takes me down ladder shafts where the rungs are slippery with moisture, and along echoing passageways strewn with skeletal remains from which patches of red crustacean-things grow. I pass long-corroded electronics, cracked and lifeless screens, and walls on which strange colourless plants grow, their worm-like roots wrapped around anything that gives them support.

Hopefully the Kchak fails to track my convoluted route. I plunge into a hexagonal room and have to squint due to the ruby dazzle. Some kind of old machinery sits in the centre, around which the most intense blisters of redness grow. They seem to be attracted to whatever this was. Pipes lead away; half-covered warning signs punctuate the surfaces. Maybe it was an engine room, or power generating system where this subterranean red shellfish species feels most at home. It's no surprise then that I've never seen these life forms before, if they grow so deeply below our surface. Many undocumented Nuafri species are left alone to exist without interference.

The contrast strikes me. This burning fire of illumination exists in the depths, never in sight of the sun, our star, which gives life to everything up above. A different order rules down here.

What Order are you part of?

The words seep into my brain with the redness, as if through my eyes and along the nerve that roots them to my core.

You see darkness, I say it is enlightenment.

Yes, it is so bright. I wish for a visor to shield my face, but my hands will have to do, pressed over my eyelids while all my pores are stretched. I can't look, but I imagine my skin is the surface of the moon, cratered, crumbling at the edges from so much information.

And I understand that it *is* them, or *it*, something in the red winks of limpet light from the tiny shells. The openings create crimson flame patterns, boosted by sentience. Existence is decoded, restrung and readable.

"Are you trying to communicate?" I ask, staggering, blind, and still the redness fills my head like blood fog.

Not trying. Succeeding.

And even with my eyes covered I can still see the walls blistered with breathing rubies, filling the space with a million pricks of light until I realise I am in space, and these are red-stage stars so far away. I stumble and put one hand out, and it touches the nipping sharpness of *not-shells-but-fragments-of-something-bigger*, something I can't comprehend.

Listen. See.

And I do, and it is wondrous.

There is nowhere to go.

There is nothing.

I am in a red hole. It is the only explanation.

There is no contiguity in experience.

Darkness in the black that is really a red, the colour of closed eyelids against the sun, but the colours are denser, further away. It's like walking barefoot in the Nuafri forest, I can feel things before I see them, despite the sucking black of the non-space around me.

My pores gape like petals opening in the sun, chapter discs unfurling for a learner, skin tingling as if plastered in kirant yellow litrus paste.

"I see you," I say.

Then what are you, *to acknowledge* me?

"I am Afua Toure." It is at the heart of the Order's training to *know thyself*. And I do. Enough to know that it is *not* my voice in my head, it truly is something else. "What are *you*?"

A misunderstood.

If I didn't know better, I would think I was a victim of one of the UFS's mind machines, toyed with by a Depth Level Five AI. We have discussed them in revisionist ethics classes at Corium, and how the AIs are suspected of mind possession like a Mbwiri. This feels like one of the scenarios I imagined, where connection allows the AIs to construct *mindlinths* – personal labyrinths out of which a victim was unlikely ever to escape. I could have crawled into a UFS baited trap, and am now at the mercy of an AI, toyed with until I go insane. Unless I am already insane. In which case, nothing matters anyway.

You passed through a door, but I gave you a key. Nothing is forced.

I am but a node on the root of the great pomark tree. I travel the xylem, drawing from it. I feel a flicker of something Mez Makente has hinted at, the trigger her acolytes need if they are to progress to the empathic stage of their training. It is the natural step on the journey of the empath to make meaning of the learning, the impressions upon the senses. "You have six senses," Mez Makente likes to say. "Use all of them."

The trigger has been pulled.

You are Afua Toure. This wisdom is nutritional. I am not artificial.

"You speak my language."

I do not. It is your brain that turns it into your language. It is flawed but it is the only way. All communication is imperfect.

"What do you want?"

You must know. About the unravelling.

"What is it?"

Was. An error. This vessel was unravelled but returned. With me and others. Most humans died. It was sadness. But they were wrong. They blamed it on me. All lies. I tried to warn them, protect them, but they did not believe me. They attacked and triggered my defences. But they were oblivious to the true threat, the OTHER brought back from the Null long journey. And it all unravelled, not destroyed. You will see.

And I am back in the sleeping quarters, but someone has tidied up. No, things are still strewn around, but they are *new*. There is light, and motion, and *this is how it was*. A woman shucks clothes off, grabbing a change of uniform, and she has a slight resemblance to myself in size and expression and I would smile, but –

A blur, then:

– snatches of conversation in an access corridor. People step smartly into alcoves to get out of the way of crew transports and cargo modules, resuming once the danger is past.

I am eavesdropping on memories, witness to history.

All true. The then, not when.

The pores of my skin expand, and my body is inflating, just as my mind stretches with the voices of the passengers and crew. Shouting and screams now reverberate from the distance, and it is clear the ship must have suffered an accident. This is history, but my gaping pores absorb more information than I can handle. Smoke floods my nostrils and I gasp, just as the crew gasp for air, shivering as black space caresses the outer hull, which blisters and buckles.

The bulkhead on my right is seared with a raised swelling, as if the ship has been lanced with something like a needle. I think of the Derago's proboscis, how it floods venom into its victims, while simultaneously drawing nourishment. The craft has been subjected to the same. And I wonder what has been injected? What has been removed? Who or *what* has been nourished?

– the spikes are in my hair, they are *in* my skin, not content with stinging and sucking, the Derago burrow deep like spiny ssanju worms and I scream –

I am alone in the dark, amidst cries for help, pleading, keening and crying, all backed by the awful sounds of spiralling sirens and the ship hull groaning under enormous pressures.

I don't want to listen as I lurch from one sensation to the next, swirling within a torrent of images, sights, smells, the tacky grasp of thoughts.

I see fire.

I am fire, glowing red with succulence, satisfaction.

No, that is a false element.

The craft is perforated as I am perforated. Filled with venom. Filled with ...

– the deck buckles as if something tunnels beneath me, and the corridor twists, tighter and tighter, the bulkhead teases into pins, stretches into erect hairs, thins to a proboscis with the buzz of a thousand Derago, until the memory crew are squeezed into atoms, screams splintered into dust –

– but now time has passed and the crew is triaging the disaster, and I catch snippets of nervous confusion, wails of pain, and the terrifying silence of burn victims who dare not wheeze or cry for fear of stretching islands of flaky skin, floating on a sheen of blood and plasma.

The unravelling was not gentle, it should be renamed, and I cannot take it any more, I tear myself away, looking for something that isn't suffering, and –

How?

– a moment of ease as I see a planet, fine sand and grey rock dotted with wiry turquoise plants. The air shimmers, not with heat but distance of the memory, and there are figures. If I press my eyes tighter, open my pores wider, I feel them. A fiercely loving woman with a shaved head, supporting a girl – physically holding her upright. This woman *treasures* the small shadow of herself, the little one she has sought endlessly, suffered so much to find. But this is all far into the *when*, further than my simple biology will allow. I am filled with a sudden sadness that I will not know this place, nor the girl, or the woman who protects her –

You are not meant to see this one. Stop trying to take control.

– I am thrown beyond the ship, into freezing blackness with no stars. A beam of energy touches the craft, flickering through all the colours of a prismatic rainbow, until the flames enveloping the ship merge. The hull is aflame, melting into strings of fiery green plasma, jarring and grating enough to set my teeth on edge.

No, let me go, let me ...

Stop it, you –

– the ship falls from the sky above a jungle planet, its hull tumbling, breaking in two. One half burns up in the atmosphere, while the second – moving slower than the front half – spins towards the surface to crash in the endless forest.

But I keep resisting. While the ship unravels, am I not still inside it, half submerged in the crust of Nuafri? Did I not crawl through the crack into the false cave?

The emergency flashes of (possible) memory are replaced with the blinking of shells. I reel under a red wave of limpets, acrid tastes on my tongue, a sour twist in my stomach, pain in my lungs.

No! I am divided because of the Others that approach, two is halved, this is not what I want, need longer to explain, unravelling, meaning, what you need to –

The memory smoke dissipates, and I am back in the room which weeps with red blinks of light. The shells have returned, and they compete with the stars in number. But unlike the memory shadows, they reveal little more than crimson light.

I hug my good hand in to my breast as if it had burned like the right, finally breaking contact with the blood-red *thing* I had grasped when I stumbled.

At last, my head is silence again.

And that enables me to hear the Kchak growl nearby, in all its hair-prickling awe.

Dooga: Random Entries From Various Lost Chapter Discs

"The morning mist rippled in front of me, crackling with the static of insect wings, as a slim Dooga snapped up forest spores, sucking them into its belly, pulsing as it grew fat. This time of day is when they are most active. I peered into the mist, resisting the urge to part it like a cloud of drapes, for it would do no good: mist is mist, and only the sun can bend it to its will. *And when it does*, I whisper, *the Dooga will be gone*."

"Dooga eat spores – moja!
Dooga eat small prey – moja!
Such as baby Derago – mbili!
Their smaller cousins – mbili!
If you eat from your family – tatu!
A cannibal you will be – tatu tatu!"

"Like Derago, the Dooga are sensitive to charged claps of energy. Both can be rendered unconscious or killed, depending upon the intensity of the charge. Unlike Derago, Dooga can sense energy charges from a distance – several lengths – and fly high to avoid them. The Dooga lacks abdomen armour, and it is thought that this enhances its senses and attunements. See the section on *balance* for further reference."

"Doogas attack not with scratchy claws, but with their heads. They flash along a path then slam into you with the weight of a litrus nut thrown hard by your enemies when there are no adults nearby. It is a mad mad suicide move, but shows they will risk everything – even their lives – when protecting young, mates or territory. Not so different from the best of us, perhaps."

"When children hunt the Dooga, it is not a killing game, but a connecting one. As the Dooga veers up to fly high, implied by the changing tone of its wings' buzz, the child wearing a palm pad can let out a sudden burst of energy above the insect – always above! – to keep its head down. The Dooga will duck, flying close to the ground. Each successive burst will force it lower, guiding it right then left, tiring the normally fast creature."

"Doogas are resilient, tougher than any other insect of its size. Just like me! And so much stamina, they can fly a full day into the wind. Just like me! And when I teach you to fly these Biti Fighters, you will too! Aho!"

"Dooga have a late imprinting trait, often resulting in strange pairings in the deep forest. Immature Dooga can be startled into *regressive survival bonding*."

The Ascent

Of course the Kchak tracked me there. They *always* track to the end. To expect anything else is to live in the dreams of ophanti, where – just for a while – they escape the hard kick of reality.

Except, this time, the dream proves truer, because buzzing from beyond it is Akalie, her litrus belly glowing. I duck behind a pillar as she circles, communicating her joy.

"I told you to flee!" I hiss.

But she is too happy. And it makes sense, now. The Kchak followed me, and she, in turn, followed the Kchak. It will have ignored her if she kept her distance, as she is too small and agile to be prey to the huge beast.

Still, she should not be here! I hope she got Tifundu out first. I wish I could know he was safe, that this was all worthwhile.

And the distraction is almost my undoing as the tooth-filled maw snaps just to my left. I roll away into a standing position and circle around the central engine-thing coated in red shells burning furnace-bright, resembling bloody blisters of molten glass. By keeping all that between myself and the Kchak, I have moments to try and come up with a better plan.

The Kchak is growling, slinking to the left, head low. I go the other way. It changes direction, one eye always on me, and I change too. If it charges to get around to me faster, I will run. It is a deadly game I play, and one where I would tire first, but it is my only idea.

Akalie has her own plan. She buzzes around the Kchak, trying to distract it, to turn it. Perhaps she hopes to repeat what happened earlier, that I will fire a charge from my palm pad when it presents its less armoured side – but I cannot! I clench my fist but my left hand is now as numb as my right. Something has damaged it, probably the contact with the red shells, and I am unable to generate and store a charge however much I focus on my racing heart. I want to tell her to stop, to get away, to avoid the jaws that snap too close. Her swollen body is far too ripe for these kinds of energetic acrobatics.

The Kchak charges me again, this time leaping over part of a broken console to land on its muscular limbs in a graceful crouch. I knock my hip on a pillar in my urge to get away, spinning me off-course. Enough to leave me vulnerable, but not enough to hide the Kchak's belly-to-the-floor backwards movement, head low. For a moment I expect a pounce, then realise my mistake, but it is too late as the quills rise. The Kchak was obviously bored of chasing me in circles.

And when the Kchak steps back, a Nuafri knows what to expect.

This is the point where I die, perforated by the heavy barbs. I see it, a clear vision, almost as vivid as the scenes from this ship's past. And yet things twist, whole histories hinge on the smallest of alterations. Some say the breeze of a flapping Dooga's wings can cause a storm elsewhere, and I believe that. Because as I stand there, defenceless, the Kchak's array raised in readiness, Akalie swoops close. Too close. She smashes into the Kchak's head, an irritation to which it responds with a casual snap that crushes my Akalie in its jaws. But that's enough to throw its aim off as I duck behind the only shelter, a heavy control panel coated in glowing red shells.

They thud into my shield so that it vibrates against my back with each impact. Heavy *thocks* that would have pierced my unarmoured flesh, ripped through vital organs like sewing needles through cloth. And I cannot stay here – the Kchak will immediately follow up to finish me off. So I stand, taking a moment to judge its approaching side so I can go the other way ... but that is not to be.

Where the quills had stuck into the fiery patch of shells, something occurs. First, a churning pattern ripples below the surface, before a thick carmine extension shoots out. It's like stretched traces of a thrown ruby, its passage overlaying itself in an arc that forms a sort of solidifying tentacle. It rips into the Kchak's side. The Kchak struggles, tries to turn, but then collapses with a whine, seeming to lose weight even as I watch. Then its eyes dull and shrink in, disappearing.

It is being sucked out from the inside. Now its ribs show clearly against the scaly skin which is plastered tight, thinning, and still the redness remains in contact.

I hope the Kchak is dead, and not just for my sake.

"Thank you," I say aloud, hoping the mind-invading consciousness can understand me, and my appreciation for being saved.

Petals bloom and stretch a nearby patch of rich scarlet. The motion attracts my eyes, which have now adjusted partly to the luminous alien fire permeating the air. And with my body so charged up for action I have time to raise my hands, trying to protect my face as something shoots towards me. It rips into my right hand, tiny fangs slicing inside in the most intense stinging since I trod on an adult ssanju worm, multiplied by ten.

Pain has a way of speeding your reflexes as your body reacts even before you acknowledge the source. Today, it happens all at once.

Tugging does nothing, I am too securely attached, and the agony in my hand must already be the beginning of the sucking process. But I do not pull with animal panic. My other hand has already drawn my razor knife and sliced through the ruby growth in one smooth cut before it can harden into true crystal, severing it. I am free. The knife drops with a clatter as I turn and run, cradling the ruined hand. It feels like the inside is minced – but the fatal sucking of fluids has been halted.

Movement slithers through the maroon flame-shells around me but I am ready this time, ducking and swerving until I am out of sight of the main patch of crimson blisters. None of the strikes hit me.

I am sorry.

The voice in my head again. Except now it seems to be coming from my ruined hand, as if that appendage was an ear. It's the red stuff that is within me, a closer contact than the touch of my palm ever formed.

"Why did you attack *me*?" I shout as the soles of my feet thump along the hard corridor, lit only by the smaller versions of the blinking red-light shells.

Blood in your body. White cells that attack the foreign agents. I could be the foreign agent.

"What?"

Cannot help it, reflex reaction before conscious thought.

The pain in my hand is agonising, forcing me to grit my teeth and making further speech impossible.

And yet, I am not lost. I remember the visions, and the layout of this ship as it was in life. Somehow I visualise the way out, like a ghost on top of the living, still fresh because it was so recent.

Or maybe the burning thing embedded in my hand is helping.

It is too much to think about.

I just run.

I am aware of tremors in the earth, as if my senses are attuned to something greater, more sensitive than before. It is the same seismic activity that unearthed this place for Tifundu to find, and it continues. The earth's constrictions are like a wrestler's squeeze. Eventually the glowing shells fade out, limpet red ceasing to weep from them, leaving only dull (*dead bye bye*) ones. I switch on my left hand's fingerlights again, pleased to find just enough trickle charge to keep me from smacking into a wall. Some routes are collapsed and closed off, where past tremors overcame the strength of hull long-strained. No one can hold up the sky forever, our legends say. The end comes to us all. It is the cycle of life.

But I do not need those fallen passages. And although the rest of this buried ship may crumble around me soon, I only need to run and climb with my good hand for a little while longer (*it is all right, you can do it, there is a break in the structure*).

I grip the hip-height gravity rails to steady myself. The metal is cool against my good palm. I don't risk unclenching the ripped one, as I don't want to see what a mess it might be in. For now, I must not faint. Then I stand on the rail to reach a crack in the ceiling, hooking my elbows over and finally climbing using holes in the wall where my toes can dig in.

On this next deck I pound my way along the grilles on the floor, crunching old shells beneath my feet. I don't remember them being so fragile, but then the ceiling trembles and dust fills the corridor. I breathe it in, cough and choke it out. The wreckage shudders as if it is breaching the Null. I must flee even faster. The earth shakes once for politeness, but does not give a second warning.

The escape is a blur. My mind is not present for all of it. Body running on automatic. The dust fills my pores, leaving me sixth senseless. I need fresh air, and soft leaves, and warm sunlight, and I am in a kind of dream in the darkness, clogged with cinders.

The corridor slants upwards as I scramble and sprint, but for the first time in forever I see greenish light. I wonder if it is an illusion at first, but it grows rather than winking out like roho, grows, the most welcoming of colours, until I burst through leaves, spluttering, one hand in front of my face, my ruined palm against my chest. Out of the dead ship and into the light.

Lots of light.

I blink in the heat of it. The bioluminescent umbrellas plugged into the trees, blazing into the ruins.

I should be happy.

I *am* happy.

And yet I am sobbing for Akalie. The thought is a kick, and I am winded, buckling on to the forest floor as everything goes black.

The Path To The Future

"Gently."

I recognise the voice in the darkness behind my eyelids. It is Mez Makente, the head of the Shanta Order.

"Give her space. Let her..."

Breathe.

I didn't know I could hold it for so long. My pores are no longer clogged. Eyes open and squint at what seems like extreme brightness – but thankfully normal (and shaded) daylight, not the red of the underworld.

I am within the trunk of a great pomark tree, the thick roots visible through the arch that has become an entrance. Normally it takes weeks to shape and harmonise a private cell from the trunk in this way, so I wonder where I am. The creamy smell of sap is soothing; likewise the soft lighting of hanache beetles with orange carapaces. I lie on a bed of spongy moss, and Mez sits cross-legged by my side.

The forest beyond our shelter is busy with people. I blink and rub at my eyes, recognise the rescue teams from Sulstar, the scholars from Corium, and members of my order, including Wendu Weike. His robes are properly fastened, I see. When he notices me waking he begins to stride over but Mez Makente waves at him – a subtle twist of her fingers, drawing the *do not disturb* sign normally reserved for acolytes. Wendu Weike's scowl, however brief, is delicious.

"I don't want us to be disturbed," she explains.

Mez Makente has greying hair, but still in the long, thick dragon tails that Shanta elders favour.

"Tifundu ..." I croak.

"Is safe."

"He told you where I was?"

"More than that, he led us here."

"My ophanti," I say, resting my head back.

Mez Makente smiles. "Mutual loyalty. He is a credit to you. Despite exhaustion, he refused to hush until you were found. Then he slept for days."

"How long ...?"

"Were you missing? Almost a week," she says. "That makes little sense, because Tifundu insisted he'd been gone less than a day. But he was emaciated, more than is usual with ophanti. And you, also, seem as if you have starved for an even longer time, so that your bones want to show themselves to the world in the contours of skin. We found you unconscious. You rambled in your sleep, and I learnt a lot that intrigues me from the words I could comprehend."

Memories return, flooding me in a ruby wave. I try to raise my hand, because I can't feel anything. Complete numbness. But it is too heavy to lift, to examine.

"Yes," says Mez. "That is a problem. We discovered the invasive element in your body, and fought to subdue its spread. We eventually stabilised it through inset freezing and containment. It is dormant, for now, but leaves you with only two choices. The simplest is to amputate, from halfway down your forearm. That will release you completely." She glances at my arm with a strange expression, as if sadness and eagerness fight in her eyes. When I raise my head slightly I just see the bulbous ice-blue cast that coats my arm, not what is within.

"Or?" I prompt.

"Or we work with you to try and control it. Prevent its growth but see if it can be communed with, utilised. We would help you accommodate in every way possible. Something wondrous has occurred, Afua. But it is your body, and your choice. And we have to acknowledge that the second option will involve a lot of pain and sacrifices. Possibly for the rest of your life. It is not an easy choice you are presented with. But nor do you have to answer straight away. We have some time. And you –" Mez Makente reaches out to brush my cheek, "if you are still the Afua I know and trained – have many questions."

"I saw things in there which weren't normal. Not just a crashed ship."

"And some of your visions were revealed by your feverish words, which conjure pictures in one who truly listens. First, eat," she says, producing a handful of belly-warming jeri beans from her pocket. Each bean, shaped like a half-moon, has enough energy for a morning hike over rough terrain. I eat two.

"Our ancestors travelled on the great ships," she continues. "I carry their memories here..." She places her hand to her heart, smoothing the ripples of colourful robes. "And here," she says, placing the tips of two long fingers to her temple. She holds them there, as if drawing memories into her fingertips. I have seen it done, once, when I was an ophanti, and I hold my breath as Mez Makente now presses fingers against the pulse in her wrist. Thin bioluminescent lines flood her skin like tributaries of a great river.

The oily juice of the jeri beans hits the lining of my stomach at the same time as colourful spores from Mez Makente's wrist twist into the space between us. One particle bounces against another, spits against a third, until the bio spores shimmer into the shape of a great ship, rich with startling detail. I reach out with my good arm, into the glow of the spore ship floating in the space between us, distracted with envious thoughts of possessing such technology.

"I remember learning about them," I tell her. "Ark ships."

"Correct. Something our traditions of storytelling have kept alive, whilst certain other cultures choose to forget – or hide – where they truly came from."

"But the creature I encountered down there, that got into my hand – was that always travelling with our ancestors?"

"Probably not." Mez Makente glances to the entrance, making sure we are not overheard, then her large brown eyes fix on me through the spore-drawn image of the spaceship. "It is more of a legend. Of lifeforms that exist in the Null. Varied they are, and the beings have many names. Sometimes wording a thing can hide its truth." She wrinkles her nose, not quite satisfied. "We refer to them politely as the Vyombo. In UFS Standard that would be Entities. Sometimes spacecraft run into problems and we think they enter the deeper Null. If they return they may be altered, infested with various Vyombo. Then they are called Lost Ships."

"I have heard those legends."

"Not legends. They exist," Mez Makente says. "And they are more gargantuan than gossip, prized for supposed wealth, and yet twisted to such a degree that boarding them is hazardous. Hardly worth the treasures onboard."

"But there are treasures?"

"More like *traces*," she says. "Whether ships are sucked out of the Null by chance or design is debatable, but they suffer an *unravelling*, that much is clear."

And there it is. The very word, and I expect *them* to enter the cell at once, to fill my head with more red tales and twists, more bloody shadows, my memory golem.

Mez continues. "The ships that return are not the same. Other times, perhaps some error or mechanism enables a single Vyombo to come into our world. I suspect that transpired in this case."

"So the red creatures I met wanted this to happen so they could come back on the ship?"

"Not necessarily. I think Vyombo suffer equally from the unravelling. That which passes through the Null, into their *space* – for want of a better word – brings as much chaos as can be found on a Lost Ship when it returns to our universe."

"Which means it might not be evil."

"Evil and good are oversimplifications from cultures that place too much emphasis on divisions and categories. Sometimes it is our responses that can change a path. The difference between a sapling being nourished, versus it being left to die." Her look has a sadness to it. Perhaps she is also considering ophanti.

Mez Makente rearranges the spores, and they become an outline of an arm, but the sparsity allows us to see inside. White dots form bones, and red ones twinkle to show something else, something that should not be in that arm.

It is my own, represented in the air between us.

Sharing tech is possible. The organic nature of Nuafri tech *makes* it possible. But for two Nuafri to share tech, an intimacy – professional, academic, or familial – is required. Sitting inside the hollowed cell of a pomark tree, talking of *then* and *when*, I feel we are as intimate as we could be. And we are alone, which helps greatly.

"May I?" I ask, reaching for the bio spores with my good hand. Mez Makente nods, and I sit up and pinch the glowing shapes to zoom in, to *unravel* the cutaway, to try and discern the contours within. My mind plays tricks on me, so that as the detail unfurls, I can imagine a tingling within my blue-encased arm, like the skin is also being peeled away. I brush other spores to one side, in order to reveal the wholeness of the crystal-like red form inside my limb.

"Clever," comments Mez Makente. "And exactly what we must now discuss. Whether you choose a clean cut from the past, to continue with your life ... or whether between us we can weave what has been unravelled into some new order."

She draws the spores back into her skin, and I blink in the sudden darkness of the pomark cell.

"A new Order?" I ask, confused.

Mez Makente smiles. "Yes. I believe so. But that is in the *when*. Like a vein or nerve, we can trace forwards and backwards, exploring to find the best way to proceed. Whether that is implanting our palm pad, or deciding our future." There, the knowing look as Mez Makente sees into me. "You have always had your doubts about this Shanta path, child."

I can't hide it.

"Yea."

"Which is why you spent so much time with your ophanti."

"They are pure of heart. Playful."

"They appeal to the ophanti inside you?"

"Yea."

"But now you have grown," she says. "You have been changed. *Triggered*."

True. And my time in the ruins of the craft raises more questions than I have answers. And yet, even half-formed, barely tangible, I have an idea about what it is I must do, and I say so, blurting it out a second before I am ready. (Thoughts such as these, I believe, are best blurted, with true ophanti impetuousness.)

"You want me to communicate with the Vyombo," I say.

Another Mez Makente smile. "Among other things," she says. "To make it your life's work."

"My life? What about my ophanti?"

"You must leave them. Your path would no longer be concerned with ninth days. You would go back and excavate the buried craft. We would call it archaeological, officially, as a historical legal cover, but secretly you would be our ambassador to the Vyombo."

My skin cools at the thought. I'm not sure I am ready to return. Or to face what is within me.

But when I contemplate courage, I think of Akalie. Her gentle nudges. The sadness that she will never get to search for the right leaf in the right tree at the right height to curl into and deliver her babies into the world. She had been my friend, a true companion. I don't want her sacrifice to be in vain. It is my responsibility to do something with the life I have been given. We Nuafri believe that the universe returns our choices to us tenfold.

"Then I choose this path," I say. "I will commune with the Vyombo. I will try to retain the part within me and come to a form of balance."

"Good. There is one more thing. To have the rights to lead an Order, you will have to undergo Thorn. After the sterilisation, you will not be the same. We never are."

"That is the path I must tread, ssanju and all. Blood is shared in all Nuafri, all life. And I will never be short of ophanti. They can be my children as much as anything from my loins." My cheeks burn at the reference, but I do not break eye contact.

"Then a decision has been made, Afua Toure. No longer will I call you 'child'. You will remain attached to the Shanta, but you will have your own Order, with acolytes of your choosing."

"Oba Mukolia," I say. More impulsiveness.

"Why?"

It is my turn to smile, and I say, "I think you know."

"Wendu Weike?" Mez Makente takes a breath. "I have been made aware of his infractions. He will be punished."

"And Oba?"

"May join you in the Order, if that is your wish."

"It is."

My cheeks flush again, but this time it is excitement, anticipation, and not least, a sense of hopelessness, as I don't know where or how to begin.

By the time I recover enough to walk, I discern where to begin. Like all stories: with the beginning.

Healers have replaced the large blue frozen cast with a smaller one, almost like a flexible glove. It draws less attention than before, since the turquoise resembles ceremonial paint if you do not look too closely.

A heavy staff of carved bluewood supports me when I need to rest, in the moments when my still-weak knees feel like they might buckle. I can plant it firmly and pull it close, leaning on it as my own third leg until the moment passes. I grow stronger by the day, but there is still much to recover.

I inhale deeply, for the vitality needed to face what comes next. In and out, like the sighing winds.

I am ready. The cautious, predatory footsteps approach. And suddenly, I am surrounded.

The ophanti – *my* ophanti – steal out of the trees. The least I can do is play to their imagination, to fill them with stories that will see them through long days and dark nights. I greet them by name, starting with Jatta and Archa, only to stop as the ring of small ophanti parts to reveal Tifundu at my side. His sweaty palm slides into mine, the good hand that does not grip the staff, his small fingers pressing into my skin. Tifundu's eyes are brighter now, brighter than the dark he led me to, encouraged me through, into the *then* and the *when*.

"I told them everything," he says, and I believe him. A glance at the faces of the ophanti convinces me that they believe him, too. "You're leaving," he says.

"Yes."

I expect a ripple of shock, but Tifundu has already laid the groundwork for my departure, and the ophanti are silent. More than that, they display a resilience I had not expected, as if deep down they understood this day would come. Tifundu has taken the sting out of it, and they are ready, as ever they will be, for desperate challenges and ultimate betrayals. They are hardened to this life, and I can only hope that the ninth days we shared might bring colour and courage for whatever their future brings.

Life as an ophanti is tough.

I should know, from my own days.

"Tifundu is right," I say, making a point of looking each ophanti in the eye. "But some things are not his place to tell." I smile to soften the blow. He has not wronged me. Rather, he has made a difficult task much less painful. "Because I know what it means to be betrayed, to be abandoned. I was ophanti," I say, and *my* ophanti lift their heads. Eleena – clever Eleena – whispers *I knew it*. Whether she did or not, I concede the point, allowing her moment, and hoping it will spur her on to push her way to the top of the community. Or perhaps to forge one of her own.

"You were ophanti?" Tifundu asks.

"Yes," I say. "Just like you."

Jatta is the first to step forward and embrace me. The ophanti follow his lead and I am engulfed in whispers, the press of small hands, and the promise of *never forgetting* and *together always*.

"Even when apart," I say.

"What about your chapter disc?" asks Eleena, holding it up.

I take it, and tap the surface, and it opens its petals in my palm – four leaves unfolding like the paper puzzles a girl makes to discover which boy she will marry. I smile at the image of blurred fingers, the snap of paper, and the glee of unfolding to reveal the name, followed by frowns when the puzzle reveals the *wrong* name. I never understood why girls added names they didn't want to marry, but there were lots of things I didn't understand. Things not even a chapter disc could answer. This chapter disc is ready to continue from the last data point Eleena had studied. I can imagine the metallic words whispering out with their stories and instructions.

"Keep it," I say. "I fear I've outgrown recordings."

Eleena takes it from me, her face illuminated with pleasure, and I intervene before snatching and fighting begins: "But there is a rule. You must share it equally. All with their turn to study, to find things out that might help you."

They all nod solemnly. It is rare for ophanti to have a disc, even shared.

"And one more thing," I say, while I have their attention. "Be kind to your Dooga. Be kind to all beings, of course: but especially to Dooga."

And then, slowly, gently, it is time to part. The ophanti are gone, as Tifundu leads them in a last chase, hunting for the imaginary beasts that must haunt him after the cave.

“Fly high, Akalie,” I say.

The path is narrow here, and yet Oba Mukolia, with a grace I had not expected, fills but a sliver of it as she walks towards me.

“Afua Toure,” Oba says. She dips her head, closes her eyes, and waits for me to touch her temple with my thumb.

It is expected.

It is also strange – just one more thing in a week of strange things.

“Oba Mukolia,” I say, cupping my hands to her delicate cheeks as she lifts her head. “We have a great journey ahead of us. Difficult. Perilous, perhaps.”

“I am ready, Afua Toure.”

“Are you?”

She nods. “Wherever you lead,” Oba says. “I am ready to follow.”

I don’t doubt her strength. Nor do I doubt what she will bring to our journey. “Our path lies this way,” I say, taking her hand in my good one as we walk. It is getting easier, and the bluewood staff is fastened to my back today. “We are to stay in the Order,” I say.

“Yea, Afua Toure.”

“But our path requires a new name.”

“The Cavanat Order,” Oba says. She apologises a second later, dipping her eyes, as if it should be me who names the Order that will demand so much of us through our lifetime. Maybe also the lifetimes of all who follow us.

But she is wrong to doubt. "A good name," I say. "'The Order found in a cave'. It hides the truth in plain sight, which is what we will have to do when asked about our researches."

"Afua Toure," Oba says. "What will I find inside the cave?"

Her question makes me smile. If Oba is frightened, she does not let it deter her. She accepts that she will enter the darkness.

It is a question my ophanti might ask, and it makes me wonder.

"Soon I will quench your curiosity. As best I can, on a subject I understand so little myself, as yet. But first: you were ophanti too, Oba?" I ask.

"Yea." Oba holds my gaze. "And you still accept me?"

The voice that is my constant companion now also speaks.

You will return, Afua Toure.

"Yes," I say, answering both at once and signalling the switch to informality.

We knew you would.

I have no reason to believe they didn't.

I squint at the highest branches, searching for my Dooga and the bright bulge of her belly, even though I know Akalie is gone. My upwards gaze is partly to hide the tears that want to brim over when I think about the past and the future. The *then* and the *when* that are at once troublesome, and deliberate. But I am not alone. Oba and I are ready to take the next step together.

Mysteries: The Cavanat Order

Little is known about the Cavanat Order, and yet it is rumoured to have a strong influence in Nuafri politics.

What does the name even mean? Something to do with a cave? A metaphor for working from the shadows? Nugallic (the official Nuafri language) is full of imprecise denotations that are based more on oral tradition and context than simple and clear definition.

The Order's public face is Afua Toure. Strangely, rather than join an order as an adult, there are rumours she *founded* the order when barely out of childhood herself. But that sounds unlikely, and is probably a fabrication, one of the layers of conceptual distancing employed by the Cavanats.

So we don't know their aims, their founding, or their goals.

On the other hand, they are a Nuafri sect, so what risk could they present? It is likely a pagan religious cult with a range of primitive practices, and from our vantage point can be seen as a beneficial distraction from interstellar politics. Infiltration is an option, but the difficulty and cost in resources is likely to outweigh any benefit.

Recommendation: categorise them as low-sec risk for the UFS, no need to include in the main surveillance programs.

—signed Sector Primogenitor, Gillesto Lainy

About Karl Drinkwater

Karl Drinkwater is an author with a silly name and a thousand-mile stare. He writes dystopian space opera, dark suspense and diverse social fiction. If you want compelling stories and characters worth caring about, then you're in the right place. Welcome!

Karl lives in Scotland and owns two kilts. He has degrees in librarianship, literature and classics, but also studied astronomy and philosophy. Dolly the cat helps him finish books by sleeping on his lap so he can't leave the desk. When he isn't writing he loves music, nature, games and vegan cake.

Go to karldrinkwater.uk to view all his books grouped by genre.

As well as crafting his own fictional worlds, Karl has supported other writers for years with his creative writing workshops, editorial services, articles on writing and publishing, and mentoring of new authors. He's also judged writing competitions such as the international Bram Stoker Awards, which act as a snapshot of quality contemporary fiction.

Don't Miss Out!

Enter your email at karldrinkwater.substack.com to be notified about his new books. Fans mean a lot to him, and replies to the newsletter go straight to his inbox, where every email is read. There is also an option for paid subscribers to support his work: in exchange you receive additional posts and complimentary books.

About Christoffer Petersen

Christoffer Petersen lives in a small forest in Jutland, in southern Denmark. He hasn't always been Danish; in fact, he borrowed his pseudonym surname from his Danish wife, Jane. Chris writes all kinds of stories in different genres, but is best known for his crime books and thrillers set in Greenland.

While living in Greenland, Chris studied for a Master of Arts in Professional Writing from Falmouth University. Chris graduated with a distinction in 2015. He has been writing full-time since January 2018.

Website: christoffer-petersen.com

Newsletter: christofferpetersen.substack.com

Other Titles By Karl Drinkwater

Lost Solace

Lost Solace

Chasing Solace

Hidden Solace

Raising Solace

Finding Solace

Lost Tales Of Solace

Helene

Grubane

Clarissa

Ruabon

Afua

UESI

Standalone Suspense

Turner

They Move Below

Harvest Festival

Manchester Summer

Cold Fusion 2000

2000 Tunes

Contemporary Short Stories

It Will Be Quick

Non-fiction

From Idea To Item

Collected Editions

Karl Drinkwater's Horror Collection

Lost Solace Five Book Edition

Authors' Notes

The Long Road To Afua

Some time ago, my wife read Karl's book called *Turner*. Back then, Jane had a book blog, and she posted reviews about the books she read. We lived in Greenland at the time, in the early 2000s, and Jane had a polar bear star rating, something I put together in Photoshop. I can't remember the review Jane gave *Turner*, and the book blog is long since defunct, but back then Karl reached out and sent Jane a physical copy of his book with thanks for the review. He's a generous guy, and it's the kind of thing he does.

I thought nothing more about it.

And neither did I read Karl's book.

Fast forward a few years and I had become an indie author, writing crime novels but desperately wanting to write science fiction. Suddenly I had a lot in common with Karl, and when Jane mentioned a post of his on social media that she was following – something about fighting to claim one's books on Amazon – I felt compelled to reach out. I also read Karl's *Lost Solace* and discovered that this was the science fiction I wanted to write. I was also cheeky and looking for an opportunity to work with an established science fiction author, someone with whom I could collaborate. Someone who was known but not famous.

No, we're not there yet. Not quite.

Karl, true to his generous nature, was open to the idea, and after slinging a few books and stories at each other, we settled on a story set on Nuafri, with the main character of Afua.

Choosing the main character was a critical start to our collaboration. It was similar to the criteria I used when I chose to contact Karl. We wanted a character who was known, but not famous. We didn't want to risk changing the voice of Opal, one of Karl's main characters in the *Lost Solace* series, for example. However, they could still function like a so-called Easter egg, so when one of Karl's readers reads *Afua*, they will perhaps remember reading about her before – really just a line or two – and be excited to discover a minor character's backstory. Of course, Afua isn't a minor character anymore, and while there is nothing in the pipeline, surely there will be more written about Afua in the future?

That might be *way* into the distant future, and not just in terms of the setting.

I started the first chapter on the first day of April in 2021. I had imagined I would spend a month writing the first draft of *Afua*, but it took me until late-January the following year. Then Karl had a bash at it, adding sections, revising others, and generally shaping it into a story that fit the world and worlds of *Lost Solace*. This took time, too, as Karl was working on novels four, five, and six in the series. I picked up my next project, and we swapped the occasional progress email along the way. I'll just add, some of those progress mails are almost as long as *Afua*.

And then, what with one thing and several others, it took a few more years to get the final version ready for publishing. The interesting thing was, when returning to the manuscript after considerable lengths of time, it became harder and harder to remember what was mine and what was Karl's. This, we both agree, is one of *Afua's* strengths. It is, we believe, seamless. A true collaboration.

And now it's over to you.

Our characters are our friends, but readers are our lifeblood. We want to thank you for picking up *Afua*, for getting to know her and her ophanti, and for walking barefoot alongside her through the forests of Nuafri, nose wrinkling as you pass through another cloud of Dooga gas. It is an intriguing planet, to be sure. But like Afua, we hope you will join us and come to think of it as home.

—*Christoffer, June 2024, Denmark*

Milton Keynes UK
Ingram Content Group UK Ltd.
UKHW030853040824
446426UK00004B/157